Samuel French Acting Edition

I0591727

The Untold Yippie Project

by Becca Schlossberg

SAMUELFRENCH.COM   SAMUELFRENCH.CO.UK

FOR PRODUCTION ENQUIRIES

UNITED STATES AND CANADA
Info@SamuelFrench.com
1-866-598-8449

UNITED KINGDOM AND EUROPE
Plays@SamuelFrench.co.uk
020-7255-4302

Each title is subject to availability from Samuel French, depending upon country of performance. Please be aware that *THE UNTOLD YIPPIE PROJECT* may not be licensed by Samuel French in your territory. Professional and amateur producers should contact the nearest Samuel French office or licensing partner to verify availability.

MUSIC USE NOTE

Licensees are solely responsible for obtaining formal written permission from copyright owners to use copyrighted music in the performance of this play and are strongly cautioned to do so. If no such permission is obtained by the licensee, then the licensee must use only original music that the licensee owns and controls. Licensees are solely responsible and liable for all music clearances and shall indemnify the copyright owners of the play(s) and their licensing agent, Samuel French, against any costs, expenses, losses and liabilities arising from the use of music by licensees. Please contact the appropriate music licensing authority in your territory for the rights to any incidental music.

IMPORTANT BILLING AND CREDIT REQUIREMENTS

If you have obtained performance rights to this title, please refer to your licensing agreement for important billing and credit requirements.

THE UNTOLD YIPPIE PROJECT had its world premiere produced by Sunglasses After Dark Productions (Madeleine Rose Parsigian, Artistic Director & Producer; Becca Schlossberg, Co-Producer; and Elena Adcock, Co-Producer) at Access Theater in New York City in August 2017. It was directed by Madeleine Rose Parsigian; the lighting design was by Abby Hoke-Brady; the prop design was by Cricket Epstein; the sound design was by Jaime Lamchick; the musical arrangements were by Jaime Lamchick and Drew Murtaugh; the fight choreography was by Grace Clower; the production stage manager was Karen Oughtred; the fight captain was Alexander Settineri. The cast was as follows:

SHIRLEY BOWLBY........................... Chelsea Nicolle Fryer

TERRY ALTMAN ....Carson Coughlin

CLYDE SPRINGFIELD .... Darien LaBeach

CARSON LUFT .... Paul Albe

NARRATOR #1 .... Alexander Settineri

NARRATOR #2 .... Elena Adcock

NARRATOR #3 .... Ashley Morgan Bloom

NARRATOR #4 .... Nicole Orabona

This production featured a very special announcement by Yippie and original Disney Day organizer David Sacks.

This play was developed as part of Ensemble Studio Theater's Youngblood (NYC).

CHARACTERS

SHIRLEY BOWLBY – (female, twenties/thirties) A research journalist; smart, empathetic.

TERRY ALTMAN – (male, twenties/thirties) Inspired by Abbie Hoffman; leader of the Yippie movement. Effervescent. Too smart for his own good. Vivacious. Sarcastic. A pain in the ass.

CLYDE SPRINGFIELD – (male, twenties/thirties) A deserter of the Yippie movement and former best friend of Terry. Doing his best to have a stable life. Sweet and loving.

CARSON LUFT – (male, forties–seventies) Should be a little older than the rest of the cast; pragmatic, gentle, sensitive.

THE ANNOUNCER – (female or male) The voice from above.

***

THE NARRATORS – (female or male, twenties/thirties) Should be a dynamic ensemble of four actors/movers, each of whom play both narrators and a variety of character roles.

NARRATOR TRACKS

NARRATOR #1 (female or male) plays **DAN GRIMM, PHILIP LETTS, CHARLIE WALSH, BARRY HOUSTON,** and **RIOT CONTROLMAN #2.**

NARRATOR #2 (female or male) plays **MARGARET WILLIAMS, KENT WALSH, JUPITER, MARTHA,** and **RIOT CONTROLMAN #1.**

NARRATOR #3 (female or male) plays **ROD TALSON, DIANNA WALSH, HUGH RAMIREZ, DUNCAN, RIOT CONTROLMAN #3,** and **NEWS ANCHOR.**

NARRATOR #4 (female or male) plays **JOAN MANTELLI, SARAH ROSENBAUM, SUE WALSH, PETE CALVERSON,** and **JD DOUGLAS.**

SETTING

Everywhere, but mostly Anaheim, CA

TIME

Then (1970) and Now

AUTHOR'S NOTES

Note on Casting

All parts in this play can be played by anyone: any race, any gender; however, please don't change the text to accommodate your casting. Since the play is set-up in a storytelling manner, we'll go with what the play is telling us. Besides, casting it this way is definitely more in touch with the spirit of the thing.

Note on Time and Form

I thought of the structure of this play very much like that of a collage. It is a collection of events, recordings, and other assorted knowledge about this historical incident. Originally, I had indicated in the text when events shift rapidly between the past and the present, or between different characters. Now, the play is written in a very fluid motion. Lighting and staging can/should help guide the focus. In that same vein, sometimes characters switch between talking as themselves in the past and talking as themselves in the present. While it may be tempting, I would refrain from playing with age too much, and while it is not necessarily realistic, I would encourage a wholeness to the characters rather than a distinction between past and present selves.

Note on Language

If you can't deal with all the expletives, I'm okay with softening and removing, and will provide a list of substitutions and deletions. Please contact Samuel French. The words are there for emphasis, and to indicate a sort of timelessness in language, but I would rather the words and the heart and the story get heard than not.

One Last Note

Indentation between lines can mean a slight pause or shift of intention.

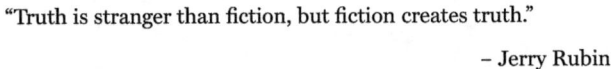

"Truth is stranger than fiction, but fiction creates truth."

– Jerry Rubin

To dad, for delivering this idea
To mom, for insisting it get done

(A bare stage.)

(The **NARRATORS** *and* **BOWLBY** *take the stage. They address the audience.)*

BOWLBY. Well, people were dying.

That's the thing that everyone forgets, for some odd reason.

Maybe that's because of the antics, or the theatrics, or this child-like sensibility – but that was because...they were kids – and these kids were *dying*. Kids were being sent *to die*.

NARRATOR #1. Shirley Bowlby, research historian and journalist.

BOWLBY. Hippies weren't just birthed out of the air, they came out of a necessity, and that necessity was: *stay the fuck alive!*

NARRATOR #2. This play examines an actual event that occurred on August 6, 1970.

NARRATOR #3. At that time in Anaheim, California, a group of Yippies, led by the radical anarchist Terry Altman, organized a takeover of Disneyland.

NARRATOR #4. At that time, they forced the park to an early close. It was the first time in the park's history that an outside police force was ever brought into the park. It was the second time in the park's history that the park ever closed early. The first time was the assassination of John F. Kennedy.

BOWLBY. In May of 1970, I began to document Terry Altman, leader of the Yippies.

NARRATOR #1. The Yippies – not the hippies, mind you – the Yippies were the radical offspring of the hippie movement.

NARRATOR #2. Yippies was short for the Youth International Party.

BOWLBY. You have to remember that this was 1970. The Summer of Love had passed. We lost Dr. King. We lost Bobby. This was all that was left. And people. Were. Angry. What was being done to stop the war in Vietnam? If anything, it was escalating! And people felt the need for a proportionate response.

ALL NARRATORS. *Kids were being sent to die.*

BOWLBY. Now, in those days I had two things I could use as a journalist: my Nikon Photomic FTN camera and this. *(Holds up a pencil.)* My journal entries, which I recorded daily, begin on May 4, 1970.

> *(Music. Something like "Everything is Beautiful" by Ray Stevens.* The* **NARRATORS** *bring on Terry's desk to transform the space.)*
>
> *(Sitting center stage, bent and forlorn, is a man in his early thirties,* **TERRY***, one of the Yippie leaders.)*
>
> *(We get the impression that this place he is in is not hip. The place he is in is dismal and he is dismal in it.)*
>
> *(He is smoking a joint.)*

TERRY. I gotta get out of this basement, man.

There's a bunch of spiders in this corner. There's maybe...eight or nine spiders all clustered together. I don't know, but I'm assuming they're all related...

---

*A license to produce *The Untold Yippie Project* does not include a performance license for "Everything is Beautiful." The publisher and author suggest that the licensee contact ASCAP or BMI to ascertain the music publisher and contact such music publisher to license or acquire permission for performance of the song. If a license or permission is unattainable for "Everything is Beautiful," the licensee may not use the song in *The Untold Yippie Project* but may create an original composition in a similar style or use a similar song in the public domain. For further information, please see Music Use Note on page 3.

(TERRY shudders.)

Either that or they're plotting. Like me.

Then there's two more over there. I just – I can't sleep knowing they're there.

I keep going back over to that spot and counting them. And recounting them.

(He counts.)

I'm like Anne Frank up in here, man. This shit is ridiculous. I gotta wait until Miep Gies brings me another book!

BOWLBY. These are the first transcripts I have of Terry. He was living in a basement in Fullerton, which is about twenty minutes north of Anaheim. The "Miep" he was speaking of was Dan Grimm, a self-proclaimed "rich kid" and longtime friend of Terry, who was also housing him.

TERRY. *(To the spiders; to the tune of "The Sound of Silence" by Simon and Garfunkel.)* Hello spiders. We are friends...

BOWLBY. Terry couldn't get out of the basement because he had a bounty on his head. More on that later.

TERRY. Does the Viet Cong send spiders? I have to use that somehow.

NARRATOR #3. His friend, Dan Grimm. This interview is from 2013.

DAN. Terry was the type of person that didn't sit down. He was always moving. He never sat down to eat. I don't think he sat down to shit.

(Meanwhile, we see TERRY freaking out about the spiders.)

He had a real charisma that was infectious. I think that's why we all followed him. He had something about him that drew you to him. And he knew how to wield it. That power.

I guess around that time in May of 1970 he was starting to get very, very bored living in my basement and...

what to do next. We were all very frustrated with how things were going. And so the idea must have come into his head long before he heard about Clyde. Clyde just sealed the deal for him.

BOWLBY. The "Clyde" he was referring to was Clyde Springfield. I interviewed him in 2014.

> (**CLYDE** *appears, very uncomfortable with this whole thing. It may take him a few moments to respond.*)

CLYDE. Friendship in many ways is sorta like falling in love. You learn trust, you learn the person, but a lot of it you can't control. A lot of it's chemistry.

NARRATOR #4. From the journal of Clyde Springfield.

CLYDE. *(Quoting.)* I finally remembered when that whirlwind came into my life. We met in seventh grade; he had just moved. We had to do a history project on Africa. We stood there in our makeshift turbans and we told the class that Africa wasn't a country, it was a continent. They didn't really get that. So, what's the capitol? No, you idiots. No! There is no capital, it's a continent. And that was that. Our defense of Africa as a continent...that's how all great friendships start.

> *(To* **BOWLBY**.*)*

We did everything together. We saw each other every weekend. We walked all over town together. When people saw me alone they used to joke, "Oh, it's just you, Springfield? Where's your twin?"

BOWLBY. So when did you hear that Terry was home and when did you decide to go see him?

CLYDE. Well, I heard he was back from Dan – I ran into him at the supermarket. I was living at home at the time, going to night school. The commute was easier. And I guess the decision was made somewhat instantly. As much as I feared it, I wanted to see him.

BOWLBY. Why did you fear it?

*(**CLYDE** does not answer. The **NARRATORS** plug in a lamp and throw down a mattress for the following scene:)*

CLYDE. There's hardly any light down here. They said you were working and I thought how can he be working in the dark?

TERRY. I work by the light of the sun.

CLYDE. *(Laughs.)* 'Course. 'Course, you do.

TERRY. Gee, Clyde, you know, you look different. Why is that?

CLYDE. Yeah...

TERRY. Oh, I know! You cut your mane.

CLYDE. Yeah.

TERRY. Your precious locks. All gone. Sorta like...what is that story in the bible? Samson? All his strength is in his head of hair and then poof! It's all gone.

(Nothing.)

CLYDE. You look good... The same. Tan.

TERRY. Thanks, Baby. I try and keep up my appearance.

CLYDE. And that hair. Taking on new heights.

TERRY. Oh, you don't have to tell me.

CLYDE. Yeah, you really –

TERRY. No. No. That means you don't have to tell me. See?

CLYDE. *(Laughs.)* Yeah.

(Clears his throat.)

How are you?

TERRY. Oh. Fine. Peachy. Dandy. Ducky. Busy.

CLYDE. Yeah, I bet. Is this your...is this where you're living?

TERRY. Yeah. Crash pad. Happy Farms went under.

CLYDE. I heard. I wondered where you went, I'm glad that...

TERRY. Dan had my back.

CLYDE. Yeah, he's a trip. Still the same old Daniel.

(**TERRY** *goes back to working.* **CLYDE** *puts his hands in his pockets. He looks around the basement, but there's not much to look at. He goes over to the mattress, sits. He picks up a letter that is stacked on top of a pile of similar-looking ones.*)

CLYDE. Is this from your mom?

TERRY. No, that's my favorite piece of hate mail. I keep it on top for inspiration.

CLYDE. *(Reads.)* "I can't wait 'til Jesus gets a hold of you, you bastard."
Wow.

TERRY. Bit of a mixed message there, don't you think?

CLYDE. Well. I feel like I should congratulate you. You're that big that you're getting hate mail. Must be from when you were on TV, right?

TERRY. I wasn't on TV.

CLYDE. Oh, I heard you were.

TERRY. Nope.

  (Nothing.)

CLYDE. I thought you'd come by the store, maybe, but you didn't.

TERRY. I'd've started to cry and then where would you have been?? Mopping up my tears of blood with your daddy's old hand sponge? Soaking and sweating. Probably would've pissed myself as well. Then you would have whipped out the disinfectant and got down on all fours to clean. Like a slovenly dog. Just would have been a sight. Too much for me; I'm a tender soul. And I'm not into such antics. Or maybe I am. Maybe I really am. Maybe I can't live without those antics. But. We all know you're not. Into them, I mean. Anymore. Thought I'd save you some trouble. Lord knows you don't want any trouble anymore.

CLYDE. Well, I would have liked to have seen you.

TERRY. I broke a bottle in front of this Pig a couple months back. It made me think of you. We had this rally in the park.

CLYDE. Which one? Which park?

TERRY. All of them. And so I screamed, "GET OUTTA MY FACE YOU FUCKING CUNT!" And this guy, terrified, right, terrified, bolted backwards – 'cause even though I was playing, totally playing with him, he thought he'd get hurt, so he backed off. And it's funny, last month, when I was interviewed I said that this stuff was hard and I realize now I should have said how easy it is.

CLYDE. When were you interviewed?

TERRY. For Dick Cavett.

CLYDE. But you said –

TERRY. I lie a lot now. Shakes you up, right?

(*Slight nothing.*)

Anyway, what I was saying was, why hire a soldier when you can hire an actor?

CLYDE. You feel like you're making progress?

TERRY. Well I'm getting hate mail so we must be doing something right.

(*Nothing.*)

CLYDE. Trent Parker died.

TERRY. Shame.

CLYDE. He served two tours –

TERRY. Well, you know what I say about that.

CLYDE. Yeah, well. Two soldiers came to his parents' house. Told his ma...she just...you could hear her crying from next door. Wailing. I remember when I had geometry class with him. First period. Sophomore year. He'd tell me to wipe the crud out of the corners of my eyes. When I think of his face, that's what I'll always remember. I hadn't seen him in about, oh, at least five years. But it's odd because...because I hadn't seen him in so long, he doesn't feel dead.

TERRY. My mom passed. Should probably mention that to you.

(Nothing.)

CLYDE. She d-did?

TERRY. Yeah.

CLYDE. When?

TERRY. Seven months ago.

CLYDE. ...But...

TERRY. Cancer.

CLYDE. God – I'm. I'm so sorry, Terry.

TERRY. So was I.

CLYDE. I didn't even... I didn't know. Nobody called.

TERRY. Well, she was in Summersville. And I arranged it, so... I could still arrange it then.

CLYDE. I loved your mom.

TERRY. Right.

CLYDE. She...

TERRY. She what?

CLYDE. I *loved* her, Terry!

TERRY. So did I, Clyde.

CLYDE. I wish I... I wish I had known. I'd at least – paid my respects to her.

TERRY. Yeah. Well. She's not entirely gone. I can still hear her yelling at me inside my head, so. You'll get it when... when your parents' time comes. You'll get it.

CLYDE. My father passed, Terry.

TERRY. Your pop and my mom, huh?

CLYDE. Mm.

TERRY. We're getting old. Shuffling off this mortal coil. Time's going quick, son. Soak. It. Up.

CLYDE. I'm soaking. But... I don't hear him.

TERRY. Not even inside the store? I find that odd.

CLYDE. I don't work there anymore.

TERRY. On to bigger and better things?

CLYDE. My mom's running it for now. I got a job at Disneyland. Going to night school, too.

TERRY. Well. Of all the things I've heard today that certainly makes the most sense.

CLYDE. I figured you might say that. But. When I heard you were home I just thought I'd come say hi. And tell you that I still...look, I really admire you, Terry, but...for me – the squatter's life – it wasn't the life I wanted to lead anymore. Okay? That's all.

TERRY. Ah ha.

CLYDE. That's all I really wanted to say.

TERRY. And the fact that your father was willing to make you a partner in his store?

CLYDE. I had a calling to do. That. Yes. For my family. But I was never gonna stay up there with you, man. I flat out told you that. And in the time I was at the commune I was so fucking sick anyway –

TERRY. Boo hoo. Hepatitis.

CLYDE. There was no doctor on Happy Farms, man, I could have –

TERRY. People get sick.

CLYDE. It didn't seem very Happy to me. And even before that –

TERRY. Yes?

CLYDE. Terry, the place was falling apart. We didn't have enough from the harvest. The water was full of shit –

TERRY. So you jumped ship. Fair and fine. But it's funny to me, man, it's just funny. Everything you were running from, everything you swore you'd avoid, you *ran* right back towards.

CLYDE. I have a responsibility. To my parents. To our name.

TERRY. And Daddy's approval.

CLYDE. Look, everything that you believe, that you *still* believe in, that we cultivated in our time together, I don't really believe anymore. With a few exceptions. Obviously. Of course. Not everything. But the lifestyle, specifically. I don't think it's sustainable. I'm pretty convinced it's not and, maybe, for the most part, criminal. So. But...that doesn't mean I don't love you. It doesn't mean we're not connected.

TERRY. Connected.

CLYDE. We have experience, man. We have time.

TERRY. When you left, Clyde, I wished that you were a go-boy for Nam. Somehow the thought of you dead in some jungle was easier to take.

CLYDE. Your jargon is getting more advanced, I see. "Go-boy."

TERRY. I'm writing my own language. And I'm calling it *FuckYou*.

CLYDE. Terry.

TERRY. You come back here for, what? You left. You went away. We were cohorts. We had forever-love. You fucked it. Up the ass. With a giant wooden screw.

CLYDE. Jesus, I wanted...

TERRY. And what? What? You think you can come back here looking like Beaver Cleaver and expect...??

CLYDE. I wanted to tell you, I'm sorry. And...

TERRY. I heard you.

CLYDE. I am. I really am!

TERRY. Sorry doesn't mean shit, Clyde. A traitor is but a traitor called.

CLYDE. Well, it's...really a shame that you feel that way.

TERRY. Groovy. Is that it?

CLYDE. You're acting like you're still on television. You don't have to do that.

TERRY. We're not? This isn't a television studio?

CLYDE. Come on. There has to be something I can do to make it up to you. I mean, come on, Terry, what do I have to do?

TERRY. You can give me some money.

CLYDE. What?

TERRY. Money. I need it. I'm short. I'm stuck in a basement. I'm trying to drive north. I need money or a car. Would you, or should I say, your dearly departed father, be willing to make an investment in a young man with great potential?

CLYDE. I thought you didn't believe in money.

TERRY. I believe in money when I need to drive up north to get the fuck away from this nasty chemical-soaked stain we call a country.

CLYDE. How much do you need?

TERRY. At least five hundred. And you're right. I don't believe in money. But willful thinking isn't going to fly me to Canada.

CLYDE. I have to think about it.

TERRY. Think about it elsewhere, please.

> (**TERRY** *returns to his work.* **CLYDE** *freezes, unsure of what to do.*)

Go please. Go. It's what you're good at.

> (*Nothing.*)

CLYDE. I'm sorry for disappointing you. Because I loved you more that anyone. You know that. But you have to grow up. When your time comes, you'll grow up, too.

> (*The scene ends, and* **BOWLBY** *takes the spotlight.*)

BOWLBY. I wanted to tell the story of Disney Day because I wanted to give this story back to the people. To inspire them. To show them *this is what we can do.* The power belongs to us. If we want to close a park, we can do it. If we want to shut down a city, we can do that too. The story was squashed for years. Because they know the truth: If this could happen at Disneyland, it could happen anywhere.

This is your story. Our story. This is an American story. And I have lost the feeling of America.

These days I feel a bit like...you know that movie, *Easy Rider*? With Dennis Hopper and Peter Fonda? Well. Its about two bikers, right? Two bikers who go on a cross-country trip. And the theme of this revolutionary, and rather trippy, little film made in 1969 is "Two men go looking for America. And they couldn't find it anywhere." That's about right.

MARGARET WILLIAMS. Well I first heard about it from the flyer.

NARRATOR #3. Margaret Williams. A takeover participant.

MARGARET. I got this flyer downtown. They had it in a record store, Marquee Records, which is where, no kidding, the giant Kmart is now. I was browsing. I was very into the movement. I was going to school, but I tried to stay as active as I could. Organized a few protests on campus. That kind of thing.

And this to me seemed like a good idea.

Disneyland. *Yes.*

We were going to attack Disneyland.

JOAN MANTELLI. I was on a bus, okay?

NARRATOR #3. Joan Mantelli. A takeover participant.

JOAN. And you know people on the bus, right?

> (*The* **NARRATORS** *become commuters: quiet, reading papers, noses transfixed in whatever they are transfixed in.*)

And this kid comes on.

ROD TALSON. Ladies and gentleman, I'm sorry to interrupt you.

NARRATOR #1. The gentlemen interrupting was Rod Talson, Terry Altman's second-in-command.

JOAN. Everyone was doing that thing, you know, *we don't hear you.* Nobody moves. Nobody breathes.

ROD. On August 6, this Saturday, we're Taking Over Disneyland. It should be a pretty swinging time. Everyone on this bus is invited. We gotta take the park back for the people. Stop the war. Bring my brother back! Bring him back, man. I'm not fucking with you. August 6. Be there.

JOAN. And then the bus stopped, almost as if he timed it that way.

> (**ROD** *gracefully exits.*)

And he got off.

I'll never forget it. It was amazing.

I immediately wrote down the date in my calendar.

PHILIP LETTS. I heard about it from a friend.

NARRATOR #2. Philip Letts.

PHILIP. I mean, it was all preplanned. The date. They picked that date to coincide with the twenty-fifth anniversary of the Hiroshima bombing.

MARGARET. We were going to attack the epitome of the consumerist, *capitalist, MECCA* of our society. They did it because it was a symbol. It still is! That's why people don't want you to know that this happened. Because if this could happen there...

SARAH ROSENBAUM. I wanted to be a part of it. Have some fun. Smoke a little grass.

NARRATOR #3. Sarah Rosenbaum.

SARAH. In addition to word of mouth, a fair amount of flyers had been circulating around town. It reached as far as Cypress College.

I still have the flyer.

> (*Flyers are handed out. Maybe a flyer is also projected on the back wall.**)

---

*Pre-made flyers are available from Samuel French, but feel free to make your own flyer, just note that it should list the date for the Yippie Disneyland Invasion, and include a schedule of the following events:

8:00 a.m. – Meditation, poetry, mantras, religious ceremony.

9:00 a.m. – Zengakureh and the art of breaking through.

10:00 a.m. – Black Panther Hot Breakfast at Aunt Jemima's Pancake House.

11:00 a.m. – Liberation of Minnie Mouse at Fantasyland.

12:00 p.m. – Self Defense Collective on Frontierland.

2:00 p.m. – Barbeque of Porky Pig and other friendly animals.

4:00 p.m. – Turning On in Tomorrowland.

SARAH. I mean, how could I not?

BOWLBY. So obviously, the word had gotten out. And it had gotten out across town, too.

NARRATOR #4. In the park. Carson Luft. Director of Operations.

CARSON. All right, everyone settle in. I know a lot of you are curious about tonight, and I know rumors have been circulating wildly, so, I would like to put those to rest as soon as I can. So. This is what we're dealing with. We received notice from the *LA Free Press* that an organization of Yippies are planning to have a sit-in, or a be-in, or what have you, tomorrow, right here, in Disneyland. There have also been a fair amount of flyers circulating around town, publicizing these events. Management and I have been coming up with a plan of action in response to this event, and we are now ready to present that plan to you all. First of all, I will tell you, we don't know how many people will show up for this event. Could be twenty thousand or two hundred or ten thousand. That being said, we have tried to plan a means in which we could effectively control the situation, no matter what the numbers are. Hopefully, it won't come to that, but just in case, we need to be prepared and take an appropriate course of action. But the first course of action, gentlemen, and ladies, is this, and say it with me now because I mean it: you are not to escalate the situation.

BARRY. And then he proceeded to dish out the plan, which was, in essence, this: stand in these areas and be observant. If you see anything, rally for your area's supervisor.

NARRATOR #2. Barry Houston. A Disney manager.

BARRY. Everyone was called in for that morning so in total there were about 100 managers on staff.

BOWLBY. What were you supposed to be seeing that you would need to alert your supervisor to?

BARRY. Anything that might disrupt the normal procedures of the park.

BOWLBY. And your supervisor would call the police?

BARRY. Well, yes, but we had members of the Riot Squad in the park already.

BOWLBY. You did?

BARRY. Yep. They were planned to be in the staging area between Main Street and the Administration Building. Not visible, of course...

I think it was the best course of action considering what we were up against.

BOWLBY. *(To audience.)* This was also the same meeting where Clyde Springfield first learned of the upcoming invasion.

(Focus shifts to **CLYDE***; he's in a state of shock.)*

CLYDE. I had no idea...

BOWLBY. You hadn't heard anything prior to that meeting?

CLYDE. No. Which made me, first of all, feel awful. I mean, how far removed was I now?

And then I felt...so...angry...

BOWLBY. Why?

CLYDE. *Because!* Because I knew! I knew what Terry was doing.

(A **NARRATOR** *brings* **CLYDE** *the phone. He stares at it. Contemplating his next move.)*

BOWLBY. I asked him later: Do you think if you hadn't gone to see him in the first place, he never would have led the Disney Takeover?

CLYDE. No, he never would have. No.

*(***CLYDE** *picks up the phone, dials.)*

(Across the stage, **DAN** *hands* **TERRY** *the phone.* **TERRY** *picks up. We are not sure what kind of state he is in. It could be the spiders or the drugs or the heat are all just too much.* **CLYDE***, on the other hand, is furious.)*

Terry.

TERRY. Yeah.

CLYDE. It's Clyde.

TERRY. *(Confused.)* Clyde?

CLYDE. Yeah. Clyde.

TERRY. Oh yeah. Didn't we –
meet already?

CLYDE. Are you...
Are you serious?

TERRY. Oh yeah! Clyde! What's good, little buddy? Why are you calling me? *(To* **DAN.***)* Didn't I tell you to screen the calls?

DAN. *(Offstage.)* I didn't know who it was!

TERRY. *(Pronouncing it Ama-Tours.)* Amateurs.

      (A beat; pronouncing Aud-It-Tours.)

  Auditors.

      (A beat; pronouncing it The-A-Tours.)

  Theaters.

CLYDE. Terry?

TERRY. Yeah.

CLYDE. You got something going down tomorrow?

TERRY. Do I?

CLYDE. *Yeah.* There's word on the street that a bunch of hippies –

TERRY. *Yippies.* God. It's *Yippies.* It's the *Youth International Par–*

CLYDE. So you are? You're planning on taking over Disneyland?
Are you?

TERRY. Whoa, Baby. Why you so mad, Baby?

CLYDE. Because...
I just...
Because...

TERRY. *Tick Tock,* Baby. Life is Tick-Tocking away while you're making up your mind, Baby.

CLYDE. I know that you did this –
Is this some kind of revenge plot, Terry?

TERRY. Revenge? I don't believe in revenge, Baby. I believe in freedom. I believe in tranquility.

CLYDE. I believe you're going to the place I work to fuck me over.

(Nothing.)

TERRY. You can believe what you want.

CLYDE. Fuck you!

TERRY. *Whoa.*

CLYDE. Fuck you, man! I got this job on a *limb*. I had *four* interviews! I finally got to bring in my own source of income for once in my life, and get away from the store, and be independent, and feel a sense of pride about my existence but now... You're taking a massive shit on my lawn, Terry!

TERRY. Are you done with your phone call now, Floyd?

CLYDE. *(Seething.)* Is that all? You're really not going to say anything about this?

TERRY. I don't really have anything to add...

CLYDE. Well, great, I'll see you tomorrow, asshole.

> (**CLYDE** *is about to slam the phone down, but he hesitates.)*

Oh, and by the way, they are calling in the Anaheim Riot Squad –

TERRY. *Whoa –*

CLYDE. – *Orange County's finest!* They are going to be stationed in the park, so, I'd watch it, if I were you. *Be fucking afraid.*

> *(Then he slams the phone down.)*

BOWLBY. So you warned him? You warned him that the Riot Squad would be there?

CLYDE. I didn't so much warn him as I did rub it in. I mean, he may have suspected it anyway, if he had any brains at all. And he did.

It didn't matter.

BOWLBY. *(To audience.)* So now, the Disney staff is prepped. The Anaheim Police are in the park and reinforcements are a quick phone call away. You can see how in retrospect even the tiniest blunder could make the whole thing blow up. But close Disneyland?

> *(A moment; the scene shifts to the park in the morning.)*

NARRATOR #3. The next morning. The park opens.

CARSON. I love opening the park in the early mornings. It's so quiet and peaceful. California mornings are quite beautiful. I think my favorite time of day, though, if we're being honest, is dusk. Too beautiful. I think God gave us dusk as a reward for getting through the day. But we have a long way to go before the end of today and we got a lot of sweeps to do before then.

> *(A **NARRATOR** helps **CARSON** run the American flag up a flagpole. It remains there for the duration of this section of the play.)*

ALL. I pledge allegiance
to the flag
of the United States of America
and to the Republic
for which it stands,
one Nation
under God,
indivisible,
with Liberty and Justice for all.

NARRATOR #4. Carson Luft was Director of Operations at Disneyland from 1956, a year after the park first opened, until 1970.

CARSON. I'm sorta like the guardian angel of this place. I get to lead the magic behind the scenes, learn all the ins and outs, run the mechanics. There's a lot that goes into this place, believe me. And a lot more to make it run smoothly. The best though…the best part aren't the secrets to the place: it's watching a family come in real early in the morning. They've clearly been waiting all night, itching to start their day. The kids are bopping up and down, anxious. Excited. Those are always nice to see. We get a lot of those here, as you might imagine. Dreams come true here. I'm proud to say it. Ain't nothing wrong with that.

KENT WALSH. Kent Walsh. My wife Dianna. We drove all the way from Georgia.

CARSON. Ah, that's quite some ways. My goodness! Well, welcome to Disneyland!

DIANNA WALSH. Charlie and Sue here are Disney fanatics. We love all the Disney stuff.

CHARLIE WALSH. I LOVE MR. DISNEY! Is he here?

SUE WALSH. *(Insanely stated.) MICKEY MOUSEEEE!*

CARSON. *Excellent.* Well, I'm so very happy for you all!

    (To audience.)

Something about that young woman screaming *"MICKEY MOUSE"* will forever remain scratched into my eardrums.

SUE. *(To audience.)* I was ten at the time.

We had driven all the way from Georgia. We were really excited.

Disney gave my family this great vehicle to connect with one another. We loved Disney stuff. And it was so so great of my parents to take us. It wasn't easy for them to do vacations. We were a pretty middle class family, but we so desperately wanted to go to Disneyland.

CHARLIE. We knew nothing of what was supposed to happen that day. Obviously, we were not informed about the Yippie Invasion.

CARSON. And at first there wasn't really anything happening.

BARRY. We saw a few kids enter the park, colorfully dressed, but they really weren't outside the realm of how other kids dressed at the time. Nothing to really flag us.

CARSON. Then around twelve o'clock, I get this radio call from Clyde Springfield up at booth ten, which was something like –

CLYDE. *(Radios.)* Clyde to Operations. Mr. Luft, can you come to reception booth ten, please?

CARSON. *(Radios.)* Hey Clyde, what's shakin'?

CLYDE. *(Radios.)* Mr. Luft, I need approval on a clerical discount.

> *(A beat.)*

CARSON. *(Radios.)* I'll be right there.

So I go up to the booth, and Clyde is there with this scraggily looking fella. I mean, really, his hair was completely insane. I had never seen anything like it. Like a giant brown spiderweb on his head.

So I say, *(To* **CLYDE.***)* what's the problem, Springfield? *(To audience.)* He says –

CLYDE. This gentleman –

TERRY. *Yeah*, I'm a gentleman –

CLYDE. Has an ID from the Universal Life Church and he would like the clerical discount. May I approve it?

CARSON. Let me see it.

> *(***CARSON** *looks at it. Beat.)*

You look familiar.

TERRY. I am a certified minister of the Universal Life Church, able to perform marriages of both a legal and auspicious nature. I hate to think Disney would want to spit on a man's religious beliefs. Also, I'm Jewish.

CARSON. Sir, no one is doing anything of the kind.

TERRY. Not yet.

CARSON. It looks okay, Clyde. Thanks for checking.

BOWLBY. Shortly after the Invasion, Disney dropped all clerical discounts.

CLYDE. Okay...

TERRY. Clyde here seems like a really good employee.

CARSON. He is. He's a forward-thinker.

TERRY. Tick-Tock, Baby. Say, I would really love to recommend him for Employee of the Month. Do you folks have an Employee of the Month?

CARSON. We do, yes.

TERRY. Oh, swell. He's just perfect for it.

CARSON. Well, thank you. I'll take that into consideration.

TERRY. So tell me, young man, what are you doing to aid the war effort?

CARSON. Yes. Well.

　　(Whispers to **CLYDE.***)*

If anything happens, just radio.

CLYDE. *(Whispers.)* Can we deny him entry?

CARSON. Well, do you have any reason to?

CLYDE. Not...

　　*(***TERRY** *occupies himself while this dialogue is delivered. Maybe he's looking at a map of the park. Maybe he's counting the tickets he just bought.)*

CARSON. This is the plan, Springfield. Until these gates close tonight, and the last firework shoots off in the sky, we are playing it cool. That is the official plan of today's proceedings. I don't care who razzles you, or what they might say, Disney's official stance is to play it cool. Try and show a little bit of empathy for these kids, okay?

CLYDE. Empathy, sir?

CARSON. Like they were your friends. For me, like they were my kids. That's my goal. And I expect everyone to make the same effort. It's the best plan, believe me.

CLYDE. Yes, sir. You got it.

CARSON. Good.

　　*(***CARSON** *exits.)*

TERRY. Exciting life you lead, right?

CLYDE. You're welcome to enter, sir.

TERRY. He seems nice.

CLYDE. Mr. Luft is a saint.

TERRY. So does he know we're friends or...?

CLYDE. Oh, we're friends?

TERRY. Well. We were. We know each other. Does he know that?

CLYDE. No.

TERRY. No. Why not?

CLYDE. Why didn't you tell him, if you're so concerned?

TERRY. Eh, it'll be more fun later. Well, gotta go. I got to meet up with some people. We're gonna hit up that Flying Elephant ride. I hear it is a hootenanny.

(**TERRY** *exits.*)

CARSON. So by mid-day, we're operating normally. No abnormalities. And not a massive surge in attendance. 25,000 people in the park in total, which is about average. There were maybe 200 people in total that could vaguely be identified as a Hippie.

SARAH. Then around three p.m. it started getting hot. One hundred degrees hot. Remember, it's August.

TERRY. (*To audience.*) And remember, I fucking hate Clyde Springfield.

JUPITER. We are going to do something, right?

NARRATOR #4. Terry's Cohorts. On the left, the woman, is known as "Jupiter." On the right, Rod Talson, the guy who told Joan Mantelli about Disney Day on the bus.

NARRATOR #1. Jupiter was an early pioneer of women's lib. Birth control, abortion, shaving, equal pay, marginalization, she covered them all in her writing and activism. And while doing so, she maintained a career as a musician. She used to say, "On Tuesdays you can find me at the Boco lounge, on Wednesday morning you can find me back on the street."

NARRATOR #4. In both the media and in Yippie circles alike, folks considered Rod Talson Terry's first lieutenant. A quick-witted, high-strung, sometimes-working-actor, he dug hieroglyphics and was once arrested on St.

Mark's Place in New York City wearing nothing but American flag boxer shorts.

TERRY. Yeah. I'm maneuvering. In my mind. We want to follow agenda, but we also want to not follow agenda, you get what I'm saying? Divert attention. Divide and conquer.

JUPITER. We were all supposed to commence on the Cinderella bridge. That was the word.

ROD. When we got there, there was a small group waiting. Young, though. A young group, mostly. Sixteen. Seventeen-year-olds. Next on the Butcher's list.

JUPITER. Terry pulls to the center of them. He says, "Hey. I organized it. Hello." One of the kids knows who he is.

TERRY. I'm very touched.

JUPITER. He starts talking and basically, we all echo it down the line.

ROD. He says, "Turn to your neighbor! Say hey!"

JUPITER. He says some of us are gonna go here. And some of us should maybe go here? And maybe some of us should do some of this, right? So, he's telling all of us what to do, and dividing us up. He says to this one group in particular:

TERRY. Hey, doesn't that look like a nice spot for shade? Sure is getting hot.

JUPITER. But he keeps it pretty casual. He says, have fun. You're at Disneyland, have some fucking fun.

ROD. So we had a good gang of us. And the longer the day went the more we realized, we had a pretty good pack of older Yips, too.

JUPITER. Waking up from their hangovers.

TERRY. *(To* **JUPITER.***)* Hey. I'm really glad you came.

JUPITER. Me too, Terry.

BARRY. So around three p.m., I observe some kids sitting in the grass. They had crossed a designated park area. They weren't supposed to be back there. I say, "All right. Time to get out of there." These kids were young. Young. Teenagers.

I radio. *(Radios.)* Frontierland to Operations. I'm observing some youth sitting in a restricted area in Frontierland. I'm gonna tell them to move.

CARSON. *(Radios.)* Roger that. Hey, Barry, just out of curiosity, is a shaggy-headed gentleman with them?

BOWLBY. Mr. Luft, just tell me one thing. Is it common practice for the Anaheim Riot Squad to exert force to keep a situation contained?

NARRATOR #3. This interview took place in March, 1971.

CARSON. You will have to ask them about their practices.

BOWLBY. Well I would imagine you would know. Didn't Disney converse with them before they came into the park? So that you were aware of their practices?

CARSON. Oh, we cooperated and communicated well with the Anaheim Police.

BOWLBY. So, wait. Whose idea was it for them to come? Yours or theirs?

CARSON. They were concerned with the amount of attendance. According to rumors, there were a possible 20,000 people coming.

BOWLBY. But when 20,000 people didn't show up, why weren't the number of policemen reduced?

CARSON. There weren't many in the park at first. The number was increased when fights broke out and we were trying to get 25,000 to leave safely.

BOWLBY. I see.

CARSON. Listen. I know you want very badly someone to blame for this.

BOWLBY. No, I'm not – blaming *you.* Not –

CARSON. This was a normal operating procedure for this kind of demonstration. This was Disneyland. With twenty-five to thirty thousand people that day in attendance. They were not going to let rioters and protesters run amok in Disneyland.

BOWLBY. Thank you. Okay – thank you.

Look, I'm not – I haven't laid blame on anyone. I don't do that. You should know that.

CARSON. Miss Bowlby –

BOWLBY. Bowlby, please.

CARSON. With all due respect, I know very well how I'm going to be painted in this little exposé you have underway. I've already been saddled with the public blame. Fired. Disgraced.

Someone has to take the blame for your purposes as well. That's how this works, correct?

BARRY. No, sir. He's not here. *(To audience.)* And then I tell the kids to move. They move, no problem. One even apologizes. I tell them move along, enjoy the park.

CLYDE. But then the second that happens, we hear Pete Calverson, another Host, start in over the radio:

PETE CALVERSON. *(Radios.)* Tomorrow to Operations.

CARSON. *(Radios.)* Operations. What's shakin', Calverson?

PETE. *(Radios.)* There's a bunch of them sorta marching with the parade?

CARSON. Be right there. *(To audience.)* Now, mind you, I am going back and forth between four distinct park areas. I'm checking in with the Anaheim Police on regular hourly intervals. I'm talking to four other main managers, but I'm also receptive to anything else that pops up. I want to be the face for Disney in these incidents. The park, at that point, is relatively sized enough for me to cover by foot and I can still run well for an old buzzard.

PETE. I observe a whole bunch of shaggy-haired youth positioned at the top of Tomorrowland, where the parade starts.

CLYDE. They're trailing right behind the Alice and Wonderland characters at the end of the parade. And then they start singing.

*(The NARRATORS sing a psychedelic song in
the style of "White Rabbit." *)*

PETE. Then they form into this conga line. There must
be maybe twenty-five, thirty people, and it's growing.
People keep joining the end of the line.

CARSON. They all look – gee, you know, it sounds stupid
but – they all look so happy. Smiles on all their faces.

BARRY. Drugged out of their minds.

CARSON. No, just –

I didn't think that at the time.

No, just – Happy.

Smiling.

Holding hands.

Some of the families in the park, the regular patrons,
they cheered 'em.

BARRY. And then they fell behind the Disney Marching Band.

CARSON. So we didn't stop them. Technically they weren't
doing anything wrong. They were holding hands and
marching, but they weren't interfering with the band.

BARRY. As the parade travels through the park they start to
straggle off. Start congregating different places.

BOWLBY. This passage is labeled TAKE BACK THE LAND.

(Quoting.)

You can take back the land. Here's how: you must
dance, scream, kick and cry at your own discretion. You
must do this in a place that the Rich owns. The Rich
have fertilized the land with the blood of our Native
American brethren, the blood of Blacks, the blood of

---

*A license to produce *The Untold Yippie Project* does not include a
performance license for "White Rabbit." The publisher and author
suggest that the licensee contact ASCAP or BMI to ascertain the
music publisher and contact such music publisher to license or acquire
permission for performance of the song. If a license or permission is
unattainable for "White Rabbit," the licensee may not use the song in
The Untold Yippie Project but may create an original composition in
a similar style or use a similar song in the public domain. For further
information, please see Music Use Note on page 3.

boys, the blood of girls. You must chuck grenades into the homes of the Rich with a yawlp.

Terry Altman, *Inside the Cultural Revolution*, 1969.

He wrote it during a small stint in prison.

BARRY. A woman comes up to me. Complaining. It's about four o'clock.

MARTHA. Sir, it's not right they talk that way in front of the children.

BARRY. And then she points to the *hairiest* man I have ever seen in my life.

HUGH. I think its only natural to be with a woman when they bleedin'. Doesn't bother me. It's a natural thang. Women be bleedin' 'cause they be *regeneratin'*. 'Cause they're strong! What do we ever do in our pitiful male lives, I mean, you know? And I know – "It's disgusting." But honestly, blood's a great lubricant.

BARRY. Sir.

HUGH. Yes?

BARRY. This is a family establishment. Can you please keep that language to a minimum, please?

CARSON. But at that point, still, it was fine. We get worse during the weekend rush.

JD DOUGLAS. I got there around four. I had a special job to do.

NARRATOR #2. JD Douglas, Terry's friend.

JD. I go up to Terry. *(He does.)* Yo man, I'm here.

TERRY. Yo man. What the fuck happened?

JD. I fucking had to get money for the fucking admission fee, man.

TERRY. I told you I need that flag, man. I was – my little heart was palpitating.

JD. Baby fucking delivered.

> *(JD hands TERRY a smallish paper grocery bag. TERRY opens it, touches the bag's contents, and shuts the bag. He looks satisfied.)*

JD. Yo Terry.

TERRY. What?

JD. I took money from Andrea's purse. For admission.

TERRY. She's gonna rip your balls off, man.

JD. I know.

TERRY. Come on.

SUE. The only eventful thing I remember before the closing are two things. I remember smelling something, something weird, near It's a Small World. I turned to Dad to ask him what is was and he said –

KENT. Peter Pan is a smelly boy.

SUE. Then there were protesters.

CHARLIE. I don't remember protesters.

SUE. Not protesters. No. People in a prayer circle. In front of the Tea Cups. Sorta blocking the front of the line. And at one point I asked my mom what that was. And she said –

DIANNA. They're praying.

SUE. And I asked why and she said –

DIANNA. I don't know.

SUE. And I asked why are they praying right there. And she said –

DIANNA. Maybe they are mad about something.

SUE. And I remember that really confused me. I asked why were they praying at Disneyland if they were mad?

CHARLIE. I remember the announcement really well. Do you remember the announcement?

SUE. Oh yeah.

> *(We hear the voice as the lights and action onstage dim for a moment.)*

ANNOUNCER. *(Voice-over.)* EXCUSE ME LADIES AND GENTLEMEN, DUE TO THE UNFORTUNATE ACTIONS OF A FEW DISORDERLY PEOPLE, WE ARE CLOSING DISNEYLAND FOR THE DAY.

PLEASE MOVE TOWARDS THE EXIT IN AN ORDERLY FASHION.

CHARLIE. But at that point, we weren't aware of the hippies, but I guess our parents were.

KENT. *(To* **CARSON.***)* Hey there, buddy. There's someone smoking a joint near *It's A Small World.*

CARSON. *(Frantic.)* I'll look into it right away, sir.

KENT. Tell them to save some for the rest of us.

   (To **DIANNA.***)*

What?

CARSON. For awhile there, in the morning, I thought it would be fine. The mood was honest to god light. And there were complaints, but it seemed manageable. And we wanted to avoid a scene, at all costs, we wanted to –

BOWLBY. Mr. Luft? I wanted to check in with you briefly. My name is Shirley Bowlby. I'm with the *LA Times.*

   (To audience.)

Which was true. I was. Just hired.

CARSON. Fabulous.

BOWLBY. Can I ask you a couple of questions about the happenings in the park today?

CARSON. Not now, Miss Bowlby. I am extremely busy.

BOWLBY. Just Bowlby, thank you. And thank you for your time. I'll find out the happenings myself.

PETE. *(Radios.)* Fantasyland to Operations. Sir, I'd love some backup for an incident near It's a Small World.

CARSON. *(Radios.)* Calverson, this is Luft. What kind of incident?

PETE. *(Radios.)* Tuning In – sorry, Turning ON – it seems, sir.

CARSON. *(Radios.)* Turning On? What are they turning on? What does that –

BOWLBY. It probably means that people are smoking pot, Mr. Luft.

CARSON. In Fantasyland?

TERRY. *(To audience.)* 'CAUSE WHY THE FUCK WOULDN'T YOU!

CARSON. *(To* **BOWLBY**.*)* Thank you for your youthful clarification there.

BOWLBY. Hey, maybe we could do tit for tat here? Please just one quick comment.

CARSON. All right – Bowlby. You know what? You seem like you're a real hip young lady, so, I'll give you something. One moment.

    (Radios.)

Operations to Koping. Koping, can you get to the entrance of It's a Small World, please?

    (We hear **KOPING** *answer in the affirmative.)*

(To **BOWLBY**.*)* We really haven't had too much trouble here today. These kids, while they may look and seem a little different, they are just like regular kids. And these are kids that care about something.

BOWLBY. They remind you of your own kids, at all?

CARSON. I don't have children, but I think we just have to take a little time to understand them. And I think if we can do that, we're all gonna get through the day in one piece, all right?

BOWLBY. Well. That's much appreciated, Mr. Luft, thank you.

CARSON. Now, if you'll excuse me.

BOWLBY. Busy day?

CARSON. Does it show?

    (Radios.)

Operations to Koping. Koping, I'm heading to Small World.

    *(***BOWLBY** *stands for a moment, looks out at the audience. Really taking in the scene.)*

BOWLBY. I remember feeling honest to god excited. It was the first time I had seen Terry in action. I'd seen him on TV, but, never in person. I believed in this man so much. I believed he was the solution.

BARRY. Now mind you, we have seen 'em all in Disneyland.

PETE. Mostly incidents of impropriety.

BARRY. I was working one day when a young employee had been fondled by some patrons. She was dressed as Pluto and a group of kids waited to take their picture with her, counted to three, and on three, they stuck their hands up her costume.

PETE. But truly, most of it is mundane. Kids throwing up on the Pirates of the Caribbean.

BARRY. Occasionally people will cut a line. Others will get huffy.

PETE. People passing out from heat exhaustion.

BARRY. Every once and awhile someone comes in a little too happy.

PETE. He means a little too drunk.

BARRY. So we have to boot 'em.

CARSON. But by five o'clock, we had only had ten reported incidents of unusual activity. Considering the event we were encountering, and the initial threat was there in the first place, it wasn't too bad. If everyone kept a cool head, we could make it out of the gate.

CLYDE. I hadn't seen him for most of the day. To his credit, he kept moving, blending in as best he could. He wasn't in any place for longer than a couple of minutes. Didn't wait on line for any of the rides. Then it's five o'clock, and I'm on dinner break, and I see, not him, but his hair – his hair bobbing on a raft to Tom Sawyer's Island. His lieutenants are with him, people I recognize. I suppose I should have mentioned it over the radio. But right then and there, they were just sailing off.

TERRY. Go back. Get the other Yips. Tell 'em we're culminating and elucidating on TSI.

CLYDE. I was stationed at the ticket booths all day, but what can I say? I was curious.

BOWLBY. I was keeping an eye out for the Yips. It was like bird sightings; you know? I spot one. And I was lucky enough to overhear him tell his friends to meet on Tom Sawyer's Island. I heard him say –

JD. Let's declare independence from the state of Walt Disney.

BOWLBY. I caught the next raft. Lucky for me, too, because when I arrived it was already bumping. That was the biggest assembly of them that day.

ROD. Before you knew it, you had about 200, all crowded in around the fort.

BOWLBY. And I got the picture.

Cover of *LA Times* the next morning.

The moment right before. It's always the moment they want to see.

CARSON. As the numbers build, the crowd starts to draw our attention.

BOWLBY. Terry was standing at the flagpole. And people are waiting around him and then he just starts talking. Getting in the zone. Getting louder.

TERRY. Alright, so why are we here? Why are we here.

> (*The* **NARRATORS** *act as the choir in this scene.*)

WE ARE LIVING IN A CORRUPT FUCKING SOCIETY!

WE ARE LIVING *IN A CORRUPT FUCKING SOCIETY!*

52,732 is not an insignificant number! 52,000 have died for *nothing!* Eighteen-year-old, nineteen-year-old *kids!* A disproportionate number of them poor, black men.

And for what? For the spread of a poisonous, outdated American dream and war money!

And the rich get richer. The poor get *fucked* and it keeps happening! It keeps happening unless YOU SAY NO!

See these walls? This place tries to take away the urgency to act. Well not today, motherfuckers. We are going to take away their right to escape.

I therefore declare WAR on the state of Walt Disney.
I declare WAR for those who cannot fight!

> (*The* **NARRATORS** *scream affirmations. Then
> all of a sudden the sound cuts, and* **TERRY**
> *talks to the audience.*)

(*To the audience; more calmly.*) Hello, my babies. Get
ready for this shit to hit the motherfucking fan.

> (**TERRY** *runs the Yippie flag – a black flag
> complete with a red star and marijuana leaf
> – up the flagpole. The* **NARRATORS** *go bananas.*
> **TERRY** *triumphantly swings the American
> flag around his shoulders like a cape.*)

CLYDE. *Fuck.*

CARSON. You could see it above the fort. It was clearly
visible. I grabbed the four closest guys near me.

TERRY. What's shakin', Mouseman?

CLYDE. What are you...

You gotta take that down, man.

TERRY. Who's gonna make me, Mouseman, you?

CLYDE. Not just me...

Terry.

TERRY. Yes?

CLYDE. You...

You gotta take that down, man.

TERRY. Say it again, Little Baby, I can't hear you.

CLYDE. You...

You obviously heard me.

TERRY. Then fuck off, Tink! Either do something or don't,
but don't stand there whacking your doobie and expect
me to take you seriously!

CLYDE. Tick-Tock, right, Terry?

TERRY. Amen, little buddy! Fucking ACT for once in your
miserable life. God, it's funny too, you always were such
a fucking pussy.

(**CLYDE** *grabs the string of the flagpole. He pushes* **TERRY** *to try and stand in front of it.* **TERRY** *holds his ground.*)

CLYDE. You are such an asshole. I'm trying to help you, man. You are outnumbered! They are behind every facade.

ROD. Who's big-man?

TERRY. Just some high-class tooter. Pay him no mind.

ROD. You know there's another raft coming out, man.

CLYDE. It's them.

TERRY. It's nothing.

ROD. Just so you and the tooter know.

TERRY. Yeah, I know.

CLYDE. Terry. Listen to me –

TERRY. Stop saying my name! Don't get in this, man. I'm taking a stand for kids who are dying and poor farmers who are being barbecued. You're standing behind the people who put them there. Being righteous is the ultimate power. And you don't have righteousness on your side.

CLYDE. *Disney* did not put them there.

TERRY. Oh no? Didn't I see Bank of America and AT&T sponsoring some rides here? Or was that just something I made up? Your system is part of *a bigger system.*

CLYDE. Terry, the manager... Carson Luft, the Operations Manager of Disneyland, is coming here –

TERRY. Sailing here, so to speak –

CLYDE. *As we speak.* And if he sees this, this is really – this is probably gonna grind his gears a little too tightly.

TERRY. Like I give a shit?

CLYDE. He is going to call across the radio for Plan B. And when Plan B goes into effect...

It's not gonna be pretty.

There are kids here, man.

TERRY. Well then, so long sweet Clyde.

(**TERRY** *turns away.* **CLYDE** *grabs* **TERRY** *and slaps him hard across the face.* **TERRY***'s*

*shocked and almost...impressed. Then it's
funny.* **TERRY** *smiles and laughs this genuine
laugh. Then* **CLYDE** *does too.)*

(Playfully.) You better stop slapping me, you little prick.

(**CLYDE** *laughs. Then something starts to
soften in* **TERRY***'s face.)*

JUPITER. Their eyes.

You could see.

Everything was starting to melt.

TERRY. You are...a dumbbell, Captain Clyde, always were.

CLYDE. *(Fondly.)* Captain Clyde. Wow. That takes me back
a long ways.

TERRY. Not so long.

CLYDE. This is not the place for this, man.

TERRY. Why not?

CLYDE. Because. Its nice! You know, it's great.

TERRY. It's *nice*?

CLYDE. This is a great place to work, man. I love it.

TERRY. Oh, Jesus.

CLYDE. Terry, people walk in here and it's like they are kids
again. Parents just stand there and watch their kids
react to things. It's so fucking nice! It makes me happy!
And its not just that: I like the people that I work with,
can you say that about yourself?

(**TERRY** *doesn't answer.)*

I'm happier than I ever...

TERRY. Oh god, man. Please don't say that.

CLYDE. Look, that's not important. What's important is
that: I know you're in trouble. You think I don't know?
Canada?! Do you think people go to Canada for their
own health?

What happened? You weren't drafted.

TERRY. No.

CLYDE. Then they've got you, don't they? They got you on
criminal charges?

They catch you and that's the end, right?

TERRY. Oh yeah.

Or not.

Actually – actually, it's hilarious. It seems – it seems I am the Invisible Man.

CLYDE. You still have time to get out.

TERRY. Don't want to get out.

CLYDE. Yes, you do. That's why you asked me for help. You want a way out.

TERRY. Not really.

CLYDE. Terry –!!

TERRY. No choice at this point. *I'm fucked.* Wanted to be free, but still so *fucked* in the end, it's unreal. What to do next?

Gotta go out in a blaze of Glory.

CLYDE. Listen, we'll...

I don't have the money, but I'll find the money. Just give me some time.

TERRY. I have no more time to waste, Baby.

Tick. Tock.

CLYDE. HAVE SOME FUCKING PATIENCE FOR ONCE IN YOUR LIFE YOU MISERABLE COCKSUCKER!

(**TERRY** *smiles.*)

What? Why are you smiling?

TERRY. Because you're always –

You'll always be –

The pride of my youth, man.

My Really Good Ones.

You have them.

But I'm done.

CLYDE. (*To* **BOWLBY**.) You know what's funny, Bowlby, we existed better in silence. That sweet silence that you can have between friends where you don't feel the silence at all. You feel this sense of grounding and belonging, like you're exactly where you should be. I felt that with him.

And I have not felt that since.

TERRY. Gotta take one for the team.

> (**CARSON** *enters with reinforcements,* **BARRY** *in front.*)

CARSON. All right, son. We've had about all we can take of this today. I'm gonna need you to take that down immediately.

TERRY. I'm prepared to be arrested, sir.

CARSON. Give me the flag and step away from the flagpole.

TERRY. I can't do that. I will, however, be arrested.

CARSON. Listen to me, compadre, I'm going to arrest you –

BARRY. But first, you are going to take that flag down off of the pole –

TERRY. Sorry. I can't do that.

CARSON. Listen. That is our flag, son. You cannot desecrate the flag of the people of the United States, do you understand me?

TERRY. Yeah, I think I get it, but if we are getting into it, you can, in fact, desecrate the flag of the people of the United States.

CARSON. You guys are giving me such hell, you know? Why don't you use your powers for good?

TERRY. Why don't you?

CARSON. I've had just about all I really need today from you guys, you know that? I'm telling you. That is our flag and you've been making hell for my staff all day. Now, you gotta cooperate here with me, okay? A little bit, all right?

TERRY. I hear you, Baby, I do. I get the frustration; I just can't take the flag –

BARRY. You son of a bitch, rat-bastard hippie, get the fuck off my flag!

CARSON. Calm down.

TERRY. Hey, fuck you, pal!

BARRY. This is completely un-Disneylike!

TERRY. *Un-Disneylike?!* You know what else is un-Disneylike: *MURDERING CHILDREN!*

CARSON. Son, you are tampering with private property. And now I'm gonna have to ask you to leave.

TERRY. Yeah, I'll leave. I'll leave after you rip my face off.

>   (*A moment.*)

BARRY. Give me the fucking flag!

>   (**BARRY** *tries to rip the flag off* **TERRY***'s shoulders.* **TERRY** *punches* **BARRY** *in the face. A bold guitar riff.*)

CLYDE. That was it. That was all it took. Because after that, I shit you not: the day exploded.

>   (*Somehow all the characters onstage show you how the day is exploding. Then* **CLYDES***' narration seems to knock us out of this momentary trance.*)

It was literally, like, all at once, everyone had descended on the island. I was like, where did all these people come from? There were cameramen?! There was the Disney staff, and the Yips just –

I remember the staff was reaching for Terry. And then all the Yips started jumping in, pulling Terry away. The Viet Cong flag got ripped down.

I don't honestly remember...

BOWLBY. Wait, but how did you do it then?

CLYDE. I don't know.

PETE. Carson has the radio.

CLYDE. I honestly don't remember, Bowlby, that's the truth.

PETE. He still hadn't called for reinforcements.

BOWLBY. He didn't?

PETE. No! He still hadn't called! So a lot of the Yips jump off the island and head north, thinking they could go back towards Main Street.

TERRY. They were stomping after me. I remember boots, stomping down all around me. But I guess I'm too quick. I end up in this tunnel.

BOWLBY. This is from *I Sold My Life To Fox Pictures.* Written in 1971.

TERRY. Disney's got all these tunnels. Under the buildings and shit. It's how we got nailed that day. They had 'em underground.

I end up walking in this tunnel.

> *(The* **NARRATORS** *transport us into the tunnel.)*

And at the end of this tunnel, there is this little station.

> *(The* **NARRATORS** *make the scene so that* **CLYDE** *and* **TERRY** *are now in that station.)*

There's a monitor. There's a radio. A flashlight.

Tiny amount of space.

A ladder leading up.

He closes the door, he says:

CLYDE. We should be safe here for awhile.

TERRY. Okay.

> *(***CLYDE** *punches* **TERRY.** **TERRY** *falls backward.* **CLYDE** *gets on top of him, starts to choke him.)*

> *(***TERRY** *kicks him in the groin.* **CLYDE** *rolls onto his stomach.)*

> *(***TERRY** *gets up, attempts to go to* **CLYDE** *and stomp him.* **CLYDE** *grabs his boot, tosses him to the side.* **TERRY** *hits his head on the wall of the tiny station. He falls.)*

> *(***CLYDE** *picks him up and throws him against the other wall.* **TERRY** *bounces off the wall.)*

> *(***CLYDE** *picks him up again and tosses him.* **TERRY** *hits the wall and lands on the ground with a sharp thud.* **CLYDE** *turns him over, gets*

on top of him, and chokes him. **TERRY** *grabs his wrists, but he can't shake* **CLYDE** *loose.)*

(Then **TERRY***'s muscles can't hold on anymore and they start to relax. His body limps.* **CLYDE** *is holding firm.)*

(Holding.)

(Then **CLYDE** *loosens his grip, softening. Trying not to cry.)*

*(***TERRY** *coughs, panting for air. He rolls onto his stomach, coughing.)*

*(***CLYDE** *slinks into a corner. He curls in his legs.)*

*(***TERRY** *coughs. He catches his breath.)*

CLYDE. I could have killed you...

TERRY. NO SHIT.

(A moment of silence and heavy breathing. Then, as if emerging out of darkness:)

CLYDE. I feel like I'm in a dream right now.

TERRY. You are.

CLYDE. I do miss it. You know?

I miss feeling like...

Like I meant something. To the world.

TERRY. You're a warrior, Clyde! I know it. They haven't beaten it out of you.

*(***TERRY** *puts his hand on* **CLYDE***'s forehead, an intimate gesture.* **CLYDE** *shrinks slightly out of shame.)*

CLYDE. Terry...

TERRY. I know what you're capable of.

I did it all for you, kid.

CLYDE. No, you – how can you say that?

TERRY. I need you back.

*(***CLYDE** *stares.* **TERRY** *removes his hand.)*

The movement is DYING. I was good for a spell, but the truth of the matter is that I'm no good solo. I burn out when I'm alone. *I don't know what to do!* I don't know what to do other than shout louder than I'm already shouting!

(**CLYDE** *looks at him. After a moment.*)

CLYDE. I'm never coming back, man.

TERRY. You might have to after this.

CLYDE. Even if that were true – the hepatitis. And having a buck fifty in my savings account. The stacks of parking tickets and eating food that's near rotting just because it's there. I can't go back to that life, Terry, I can't.

TERRY. I'm still here. Still alive. And it ain't so bad.

CLYDE. You could surrender, too, you know? No one's forcing you to do this! You could join me on the other side!

TERRY. And give up the gut? That gut – is the most beautiful thing there is – that gut, lizard thing! He fights the demons, man! He fights the clock.

CLYDE. But there's also...you know...peace? There's a life that's just work and home and satisfaction. In my head, I at least know that I am doing something that's honest. And that's...

TERRY. Easy?

CLYDE. It's a lot harder than you think.

TERRY. I can't do that, man. I can't – you have to stop asking for something you can't have. And you know what? I have to stop asking too. And that's it. Okay? That's it.

CLYDE. That's not it.

I'm going to ask you something and I want you to answer me honestly.

TERRY. Whoa. Honesty. That's a fun concept –

CLYDE. Will you just drop the *fucking bullshit* for thirty seconds and answer me honestly!

TERRY. What?

CLYDE. Do you respect me?

TERRY. What kind of a question is that? You don't need my respect.

CLYDE. Do you love me then?

TERRY. Clyde.

CLYDE. Do you?

TERRY. You don't need either of these things from me!

CLYDE. If neither of us can change, then fine. I'll accept that. But I cannot accept the idea that just because of that, we can't love each other anymore. That's all I want, Terry, I just – I just want that to be true. I... I really need that to be true. Just so I know that at least at one point I meant something. To someone. Can you please just give that?

TERRY. But I can't –

CLYDE. What?

TERRY. I can't

love someone

I don't respect...

(A moment. This is sinking in.)

CLYDE. And you don't respect me because I work here?

TERRY. Correct. I think you work here to convince yourself that you're somehow different than your father. And it's bullshit.

CLYDE. *(Seriously hurt.)* Well, that's not true, but – what is true is that you really love your ideas more than you love people.

TERRY. What?

CLYDE. You don't care who gets hurt. Whatever you say is whatever you say. You know what, man? Hold tight to those ideas because they're going to be the only things keeping you warm when you're left out in the cold.

(A moment.)

TERRY. Okay, you know what? Let's just wait for the cops to come.

BOWLBY. So when was the decision to close the park made?

CARSON. Well, after that, a bunch of the Yips started panicking. They charged back towards Main Street, trying to get momentum. They circle around the Main Street flagpole, singing "Kumbaya." Or something. I remember them chanting, ya know, "Liberate Minnie!"

BOWLBY. So, that was when the Riot Squad came –?

CARSON. No. Our regular customers were mad at that point. The Yips had flung themselves down the street. And when they started chanting, people start singing back.

> (The **NARRATORS** angrily sing "God Bless America."*)

> (**CARSON** starts to speak over them as they finish.)

CARSON. This whole group of guests, like, 400 people! So then the Yips get discouraged by that. They break the circle. And they walk all dejected up Main Street, back towards the park. At that point, I'm there to block them off.

> (**CARSON** appears before a line of Yips. He looks way worse for wear.)

Fellas, there will be no more marching, no more singing, no more smoking. If you are going to be here, you are going to enjoy the park and nothing else.

And one says –

DUNCAN. HEIL DISNEY!

---

*A license to produce *The Untold Yippie Project* does not include a performance license for "God Bless America." The publisher and author suggest that the licensee contact ASCAP or BMI to ascertain the music publisher and contact such music publisher to license or acquire permission for performance of the song. If a license or permission is unattainable for "God Bless America," the licensee may not use the song in *The Untold Yippie Project* but may create an original composition in a similar style or use a similar song in the public domain. For further information, please see Music Use Note on page 3.

CARSON. I hold my ground. And he punches me. Square in the chin.

>   (**DUNCAN** *punches* **CARSON.**)

Son of a –!

BOWLBY. So, that's when you –?

CARSON. I had truly hoped it wouldn't come to this. But you know what? I was wrong. At that point, I was furious, too – So mad I was seeing red.

BOWLBY. So did you call for backup, or...?

CARSON. At that point, I felt I had no choice.
> So the Riot Police came. And they took over from there. They swept on in, they called for the close. They managed the street situation which was easy because they came out from the Castle. Just kept – piling them on in.

BOWLBY. They could come out from the Castle?

CHARLIE. And all of a sudden we hear the announcement:

ANNOUNCER. *(Voice-over.)* EXCUSE ME LADIES AND GENTLEMEN, DUE TO THE UNFORTUNATE ACTIONS OF A FEW DISORDERLY PEOPLE, WE ARE CLOSING DISNEYLAND FOR THE DAY. PLEASE MOVE TOWARDS THE EXIT IN AN ORDERLY FASHION.

SUE. The attendants start marching us towards the exit. I don't understand what's happening.

CHARLIE. Our parents don't really tell us what's going on, but they got some pretty serious faces on. I remember telling them I don't want to leave the park. Please! You know, why are they shutting the park?

SUE. Mom and Dad were disappointed, too. Really, really disappointed.

CHARLIE. And at first it was fine. People were staying calm. Then the closer we get to the exit –

SUE. The crowd doubles.

CHARLIE. People start getting pushy.

SUE. I was scared. Really scared. I had never experienced anything like that before. We grew up in a town with a population of 430 people. I had never been around crowds like that.

CHARLIE. It was so devastating for us. We were supposed to go to Disneyland to have fun, you know, and then this ends up happening. I mean, obviously there were things going on. I'm old enough now to understand it, but at the time I was just like, destroyed by having to leave.

It was my happy place, you know?

BOWLBY. The Riot Police were lined up along Main Street. I couldn't believe it. It was such a *sight*, you know? A line of Anaheim Riot Squad across Sleeping Beauty's Castle.

I'm snapping photos like crazy. I have no idea where Terry is. And I keep moving, right, I'm listening and trying to take notes. So they are clearing the park section by section. But some of these individual teams I see go after some of the stragglers. And these guys are huge, okay? They got the padded vests, yard-long batons. They were terrifying fuckers. Like, if they were coming after me, I'd shit my pants.

Oh, god, and then this other group! This other Squad tries to force some of the Yips out of the park. So the Yips charge them, try to break through. That didn't work out so hot.

I'll never forget this. These two Squad men threw this kid down and they hit him five times. These hard hits.

(The NARRATORS create this.)

BOWLBY. One.

Two.

Three.

Four.

Five.

The crowd's shaken. They pick him up and I remembered thinking immediately that they must have broken all the bones in his hand.

It was just sorta hanging there by the skin.

Terry said of all riots in *Burn the Smelly Establishment*: "The kind of treatment towards us long hairs is one that has long been reserved for blacks."

Then I turn, and the Squad were bringing people they were arresting into this back area behind the Mickey Mouse Stage. I guess they wanted to keep them away from the other patrons and the other protesters. Divide and conquer.

They've made maybe twenty arrests.

BARRY. Squad should handle this lot. But they told us to get to the perimeter position.

CARSON. What the hell was that, Barry?

BARRY. What was what, sir?

CARSON. You know exactly what, don't you, Barry! I told all staff that we were not to escalate the situation!

BARRY. They were never gonna take that flag down!

CARSON. You know, Barry, I can deal with your trigger-happy self on any other day, except today!

BARRY. Mr. Carson, with all due respect, I don't even really feel like it's my fault.

CARSON. What are you –? You made an aggressive action, Barry! The first aggressive action!

BARRY. I was defending the integrity of this place. That's all. I was not going to let that ignorant Jew-fuck hold his ground.

CARSON. *Jew-fuck?!* What are you talkin' –? He's not even Jewish, Barry!

BARRY. Yes, he is, sir! Look it up! *They're all fucking Jews!*

CARSON. You're done after this, Barry. I hope you know.

BARRY. I'm done? Yeah, okay. If you ask me, sir, I think a lot of people around these parts feel like you should be doing more. I at least acted!

CARSON. I'm still your superior, Houston. And I say, goodbye. Right now. Leave with the rest of the crowd. I do not want to see you wearing that uniform.

Talk about Un-Disneylike.

(After a tense moment, **BARRY** *leaves. A* **RIOT CONTROLMAN** *goes to* **CARSON**.*)*

RIOT CONTROLMAN #1. Mr. Luft.

(The **RIOT CONTROLMAN** *hands* **CARSON** *a thin, steel pole.)*

CARSON. What's this?

RIOT CONTROLMAN #1. For the stragglers. Please go to the perimeter.

CARSON. No, I'm going on the sweeps. They need me for security.

*(***CARSON** *hands him the pole back.)*

ROD. They broke my coccyx that day. That was the day that they broke my coccyx.

Fun fact about that day: we brought a few flags with us. The Viet Cong flag among them. Pretty out of sight! So I hang it up on this entranceway. And some clean-cut, Nazi-looking pedestrian rips it down. I get really pissed and I jump him.

(A **NARRATOR** *lifts* **ROD** *from behind and tosses him backwards. Then he stomps on* **ROD**'s *back with his big old boot.* **JUPITER** *tries to stop it and is hit in the stomach.* **SARAH** *has just witnessed this.)*

SARAH. Miss, are you okay?

JUPITER. *(Holding her stomach.)* I think I have to get to a hospital.

SARAH. Well, I'll lead you to the front. They'll take you to the hospital.

JUPITER. No! They won't. I don't want them to – I just need to walk it off. That was my friend. Shit. I don't know what to do.

SARAH. It's okay. It's gonna be fine.

RIOT CONTROLMAN #1. MOVE TO THE FRONT, please!

JUPITER. You're pretty all right. What's your name?

SARAH. Sarah.

JUPITER. Sarah. Thanks for helping me. I'm Jupiter.

SARAH. That's your name?! That's amazing.

RIOT CONTROLMAN #1. MOVE QUICKLY, please!

JUPITER. You know what the benefit of being a woman is at these things, Sarah?

SARAH. What?

JUPITER. The cops don't usually arrest you first. And that's something that one could use to their advantage, like if, let's say, we exited into the parking lot and regrouped there?

SARAH. That's an excellent idea.

JUPITER. *(To audience.)* So we regroup there and end up going to the Disney hotel. That's when me and a few others got arrested. They were rough. I told them I was pregnant. They *did not* care. They could not give less of a shit. They knocked me all around. It was painful. It's kind of amazing I didn't lose Alistar. Wanna hear something that's kinda crappy?

BOWLBY. I'm sure it's not.

JUPITER. I was on the fence about the pregnancy and the fact that the baby made it that day just seemed like all the more reason...

BOWLBY. Oh wow.

JUPITER. Its just interesting the things we let shape our lives, you know?

DIANNA. We were stuck in that parking lot for two hours. Everyone leaving all at once. My god, it was a nightmare. And it was all still an active warzone, basically.

CARSON. A lot of the Yips were forced out at that point, but some of the hardcore ones were ripping up flowerbeds and tromping through the cars.

KENT. When we finally got back to our hotel, the Disney hotel, it still wasn't over! There were cop cars waiting there. They were waiting on this group of hooligans marching towards it. They had them cut off basically at that point. There was nowhere to hide.

DIANNA. So we get the kids inside, you know? We all just sat in the lobby of the hotel. In shock, I suppose.

KENT. They gave us complimentary tickets to come back the next day but I had to get back to work.

DIANNA. The kids were so sad. We were all so sad.

KENT. We ordered some room service. I said, "Hey, anybody want some room service?" You know, trying to cheer everyone up.

I got Charlie to smile that night. I dipped my fries in my milkshake. He had never seen that before. And I got Sue to smile that night, too. I did some impression of one of the characters? I can't remember which?

DIANNA. Oh, honey bear, yes, you do!

KENT. Oh, I don't –

DIANNA. Honey bear, do it!

KENT. It's embarrassing.

DIANNA. Oh, please! It's so good!

KENT. I don't –

DIANNA. Show her!

(*After a moment of* **KENT** *deciding…*)

KENT. (*Doing his best impression.*) Jiminy Cricket! That got her going, you know. That was all I really wanted to do, at that point…to make her smile.

CARSON. Our main concern was that we still didn't have everybody. We had to clear out the area. It took hours and hours and Team after Team. We had to turn the sprinklers on to get them out from hiding!

RIOT CONTROLMAN #2. Oh, look! There's two more of them in here!

BOWLBY. When did you encounter Mr. Altman?

CARSON. Ah, it wasn't too long.

RIOT CONTROLMAN #3. Two in here!

RIOT CONTROLMAN #1. Let's go. Hands in the air!

> (**CLYDE** *and* **TERRY** *put their hands in the air as the* **CONTROLMEN** *point their sticks in the men's faces.*)

RIOT CONTROLMAN #2. What is this place? The Disney vault?

CARSON. Hold it. Hold it.

> (**CARSON** *approaches* **CLYDE.**)

Wait wait, he's with us. He's a Disney employee – Springfield, what are you doing in here?

RIOT CONTROLMAN #1. Wait. Wait wait.

This is Altman.

RIOT CONTROLMAN #2. Who?

RIOT CONTROLMAN #1. The leader, you fucking idiot, you have a flyer about him in your pocket.

RIOT CONTROLMAN #2. *(Remembering.)* Oh shit!

CARSON. Terry Altman? That's why your face –

TERRY. Seen me before, Doc?

CARSON. Well, yes, as a matter of fact, I have. Prior to this day, I saw you interviewed on television, Mr. Altman.

TERRY. Terry, man, please.

RIOT CONTROLMAN #3. *(Reading a flyer from his pocket.)* It seems you're also wanted for resisting, possession of drugs, conspiracy with intent to incite riot (huh, look's like there will be two of those offenses by the end of today) and assaulting a police officer.

TERRY. Anything you say can and will be held against me in a court of law.

CARSON. You lead a busy life.

TERRY. Tick Tock.

CARSON. What?

TERRY. I said Tick Tock, Baby. Gotta keep busy.

CARSON. You said – what did you say on Merv Griffin? Someone from the crowd asked you why you call policemen pigs. What did you say?

TERRY. 'Cause on TV we can't call them cocksuckers?

CARSON. Right. That's it.

(*They handcuff* **TERRY.** **CLYDE** *visibly twitches.*)

How'd you get him in here, Springfield?

RIOT CONTROLMAN #1. I want him outta here. It'll squash morale.

TERRY. You can't stop the magic, Baby. This machine is finely-tuned and already rolling down the sidewalk.

CARSON. That's really how you talk, huh?

RIOT CONTROLMAN #3. (*Radios.*) Team C, we've apprehended a Leader, we're bringing him up now. We're on the sub surveillance level.

CARSON. Yes, well, dopey of me to think otherwise –

TERRY. Grumpy of you to suggest.

(*We hear the voice of one of the* **RIOT CONTROLMEN** *over the radio, "Roger back."*)

RIOT CONTROLMAN #1. Let's go.

CLYDE. Sir, I didn't –

CARSON. What?

CLYDE. I don't know. Nothing. I don't know.

CARSON. What don't you know, Clyde?

CLYDE. He was my friend – he was my friend from when I was a kid. I'm sorry, I just – that's what happened. I didn't want it to happen like that, but then it happened like that.

CARSON. Wait a minute.

Oh, I see.

So you two are buddies. And you were hiding him?

CLYDE. Not hiding, not –

CARSON. You were…Turning On?

CLYDE. Not – I mean, no – what's that again?

TERRY. Kill me.

CARSON. Funny, though.

CLYDE. What?

CARSON. He's a homegrown boy. Like you.

CLYDE. Yeah.

CARSON. Well, that's just perfect.

RIOT CONTROLMAN #1. Mr. Luft, we're going to bring him up now.

> (**CARSON** *nods as the* **CONTROLMEN** *exit with* **TERRY.**)

CARSON. We gave you kids everything, do you know that?

TERRY. Oh, Christ.

CARSON. We gave you things that I could only *dream* about as a young person.

TERRY. Oh, yes, sir!

CARSON. Wait! Stop.

> (*They stop.* **CARSON** *turns* **TERRY** *toward him.*)

You don't have a speck of gratitude?

TERRY. You did do that and you know what, Mr. Luft? Have you ever thought that maybe that was part of the problem?

CARSON. What do you mean?

TERRY. I mean simply that you created a generation that you told to follow their own heart. Did you not think, hey, maybe one day this may wake up and bite us in the ass?

You made us, Mr. Luft. I am a product of my times. And I'm not gonna let you kill your mistakes!

CARSON. We gave you the dream! It's a dream worth protecting! We gave you *everything* and you made your own mistakes, terrible ones. That was not our fault!

TERRY. No, no, no, sir. You gave us a world in which we could live free. There is a cost to that world.

(CARSON instinctively, and without any restraint, punches TERRY in the stomach, hard. TERRY coughs and doesn't stop coughing.)

CARSON. *(Horrified.)* Oh, Jesus. Jesus – get him out of here!

CLYDE. Terry? Terry, are you okay?

(The CONTROLMEN exit with TERRY, who is still violently coughing.)

Mr. Luft.

CARSON. Please leave, Clyde. I don't think I have to say this aloud, but please don't come back to work tomorrow.

CLYDE. Sir, he's my oldest friend, I – You think it's that easy to throw someone like that to the fucking wolves?!

I can't – please, sir, I love this place.

CARSON. Then you should have worked harder to protect it.

(CLYDE leaves.)

(CARSON takes a moment. Rubs his hand.)

(Then he starts to cry.)

NARRATOR #1. They raided the rest of the property: Fantasyland, Tomorrowland, Frontierland, Adventureland.

NARRATOR #2. Going in and getting the Yips.

NARRATOR #3. The Sick in The Heads.

NARRATOR #4. Hiding in locker rooms and in the rides.

NARRATOR #1. And as they pulled Terry through the park and snapped his photograph –

TERRY. *(As he is being dragged off and the photo is being taken.)* BREATHE DEEP BABY BOOMERS!!

(TERRY collapses into coughs.)

CARSON. Why did you care so much about them?

BOWLBY. Excuse me?

CARSON. Why did you care so much about them?

BOWLBY. I thought this was my interview?

CARSON. Funny, I thought it was a discussion.

BOWLBY. Mr. Luft. I probably shouldn't be telling you my personal views on this whole thing.

CARSON. Why not?

BOWLBY. It doesn't feel appropriate. It will pollute your opinion.

CARSON. Were you in love with the guy?

BOWLBY. Who? *Terry?*

CARSON. Yeah, Mr. Altman.

BOWLBY. No. No no. I just – and that would be – I mean, who asks that to someone!

CARSON. I think it's a fair question.

BOWLBY. No! Goodness, no. No! I just –

CARSON. Then explain to me why someone like yourself, who is clearly an intelligent person was drawn into this whole mess?

BOWLBY. I'm a little offended that you think I would join this movement just for Terry.

CARSON. Then I apologize! Please. I have spent – many days thinking about this incident, so, I would appreciate if you could shed some light.

BOWLBY. It was quite simple, really. I saw a Yippie, his name was David Sacks, speak at the University of Wisconsin. And he got onstage, and he looked out at the crowd, and he smiled and he said – I'll never forget this – he just halted, very still, and looked at the crowd and he said,

"I'm taking you all in.

And I appreciate you and love you for being here."

And he meant it.

And that was it.

That was the movement to me.

Terry helped cradle that movement. And he isn't perfect, but. He is all we have. And at least he is doing it.

CARSON. So you loved it for the connection it promised?

BOWLBY. Yes, I didn't know you could...look at people like
that. Love people like that. I needed –
Someone to look at me like that.

CARSON. And do you think your friends, these people, who
advocated this type of unity, were in direct contradiction
to that avocation based on their behavior that day?
Don't you think that they created an unnecessary
display of violence?

BOWLBY. I think they were standing up for what they
believed, with whatever means necessary.

CARSON. Oh, come on now, Bowlby.
Connection.
It means honesty.

BOWLBY. *(Hesitates.)* Yes, I think it is quite possible that they
did that.

CLYDE. The story was covered all over the West Coast. But
back in those days, news wasn't instant. The story was
mostly contained to that area. The one thing that was
focused on more than anything else was Terry's arrest.
Then word came in about a week later he was being
indicted for inciting a riot. Again. That was two counts
in two years. So. He really was screwed.

BOWLBY. Disney also installed a new policy. Long hairs
were no longer allowed into the park. Those who
maintained, and I quote, "only the cleanest and strictest
grooming practices" would be admitted.

PETE. That was a scary time afterwards, too, because –
we didn't know what to do. The next day we had the
Anaheim Police stationed at every entrance.
Less than three months later, we had a Grand Funk
Railroad rock concert at the Anaheim Convention
Center. And after the concert, the crowd started to
wander into the Disney parking lot.
On Disney Day, there were 300 members of the Riot
Squad, in total. And as you know, it didn't go so hot.
They got so paranoid from the Yippie event that when

the concert happened, they sent in *400* officers. They grinded up those poor kids into lunch meat.

It was – it was, really, it was a rough few months for us.

CLYDE. It was a rough time for everybody.

(*The* **NARRATORS** *set up two chairs.* **TERRY** *and* **BOWLBY** *sit.*)

BOWLBY. They said your bail is set at fifty thousand.

TERRY. Mm.

BOWLBY. Terry?

TERRY. Mm.

BOWLBY. Are you okay?

TERRY. Mmm.

BOWLBY. Are you discouraged?

TERRY. What?

BOWLBY. You seem off. Is something wrong?

TERRY. Discouraged…

BOWLBY. Yeah. You're not talking.

TERRY. Don't feel like talking.

BOWLBY. Is something happening to you in here?

Terry?

Look, let's change the subject. Can you tell me about after you arrived in the station?

TERRY. Bowlby.

BOWLBY. Yeah?

TERRY. Are you gonna remember us?

I mean, in like, fifty years?

BOWLBY. What?

TERRY. Nothing.

BOWLBY. Terry, look –

You just did the impossible. You made national headlines. Your message is heard. I mean, isn't that what this is all for? That's what matters the most.

(*A beat.*)

And besides, everything's gonna be okay.

TERRY. *(Near tears.)* Ughhh, *man,* I wish that were true.

CLYDE. But to my surprise, Terry made bail. Someone must have come in there at the last minute and...maybe it was his dad. I don't know. I always kind of hoped it was his father bailing him out in the end. They set his court date for February of the upcoming year. But the day comes, and he doesn't show up.

NEWS ANCHOR. Terry Altman, the leader of the Yippies, a counterculture movement protesting the war in Vietnam, has been reported missing by authorities. Mr. Altman failed to present himself in court on the day of his hearing this Sunday for crimes against the federal government.

CLYDE. So now he's a fugitive. He's on the run. Where is Terry Altman?

ROD. Our network was tight. Nobody cracked. And nobody could find him.

CLYDE. I check the papers every day, but – nothing.

Pretty great, right? I mean, some real Agatha-Christie-type-of-shit.

BOWLBY. So then what happens?

CLYDE. Well, then a year goes by.

Then five years go by.

A lot happens to me, personally, you know, I get married. I have my first child, a daughter. I'm living this nice, quiet but cool life. Back at the store, by the way, that's where I ended up after Disneyland didn't work out.

BOWLBY. Oh, you did?

*(**CLYDE** shrugs.)*

CLYDE. It wasn't so bad. My mom was grateful. And I think the girls are gonna keep it going, too.

Anyway, then August rolls around.

It's been six years since Terry disappeared.

And I get this letter.

(He shows it to the audience.)

No stamp on it. Just a letter.

(He opens it.)

And the letter says,

Dear Clyde,

If this letter has reached you...

(He stops himself, overtaken. **TERRY** *continues for him.)*

TERRY. If this letter has reached you that means you probably know who wrote it, and still decided to open it. So, that's good. Good for me, anyway.

Hello, Captain Clyde.

This is a tough letter to begin. How can I sufficiently fill you in on the last six years in one sentence? I don't think I am that talented. Shocking, I know.

In these past six years, I have traveled to nearly every state. Some observations:

One. The Dakotas are better than you'd think.

Two. Wyoming sucks some real tail, and

Three. In Kansas there's nothing to do but watch all the flatness be flat.

I have even been to other countries, posing as a food critic for a while as I toured through Europe.

(He collapses into laughter at the absurdity of this fact.)

(I really am the Invisible Man!)

CLYDE. That part's in parentheses.

TERRY. I change identities every few months, the product of an elaborate network I put in place before I left. I pick up a phone, say they're on to me, I'm told a new location, and I'm met with a friendly smile and a new name. And I've been doing it every few months for the past six years. I wonder how much longer a man could keep doing this. Because you could, Clyde. You could do it forever.

And maybe I would if it weren't for this little thing, this *little* little thing: Jupiter bore our son in 1971. I don't know if you heard about that.

But I've never seen him.

I can't see my own son. I can't hear his voice. I cannot smell his hair.

Lately, to tell you the truth, I can't sleep. I just lay awake, restless, high as a fucking kite, staring at the door, knowing they'll come. *Knowing* they'll find me.

I'm living in that paranoia. I feel myself becoming old. Feeling this ticking. This constant ticking. I think sometimes for hours. I stir and stew and become mangled by my own thoughts, thoughts that used to grow into something else, something far more beautiful than what they have become.

I ache for something familiar. And that might be why...

Why it's you. You might want to know. Why am I telling you this? It's not because I think you'll be celebrating it, actually.

It's because I somehow believe you still would want to know.

To ask for your forgiveness would be an impossible thing, but I still wish to ask for it. I treated you unconscionably. And in case you're wondering, it haunts me. You were probably the only real friend I've ever had and I threw you in the mud.

The truth is that I did – I do love you more than ideas – that has been the long, painful revelation; revolutions don't live in ideas, they live in people.

I lost the revolution, kid. I lost it and I'll never get it back.

But I can at least ask for your forgiveness. Before the end.

I hope to see your face again, dear Clyde.

Your long-lost friend,

Terry.

BOWLBY. And how did you respond?

(A moment.)

CLYDE. I didn't.

NARRATOR #3. Terry Altman re-emerged in 1977.

NARRATOR #4. And from there, it got better.

NARRATOR #1. He acted as his own defense attorney in his long-anticipated court hearing. His main defense: the necessity for revolutionaries.

NARRATOR #2. The war, now over, was looked back upon with regret by most Americans.

NARRATOR #3. And so when all was said and done, he served only about a year in prison.

JUPITER. He thought maybe that he would have been forgotten in all that time. No one forgot about Terry Altman.

NARRATOR #4. After his release from jail, he spent some time down in South Africa, fighting the apartheid.

NARRATOR #1. He spent some time in South America protesting American involvement in environmental affairs.

NARRATOR #3. He was also one of the early advocates of universal health care.

CLYDE. And in all that time, I still hadn't sent my reply.

BOWLBY. Why?

CLYDE. I don't know. Thing is though, I had forgiven him. I really had. In my heart, he was already forgiven. I just didn't want to tell him. I think part of me needed to show him that I had chosen the right life, that I didn't need him. Then I realized I was just doing – the same thing I had accused him of years earlier. So I finally draft my reply. And then, right at that exact moment, god, it was almost cosmic...

NEWS ANCHOR. Terry Altman, activist, and founder of the Yippie movement, a movement dedicated to ending the war in Vietnam, is dead. He was found dead near his home in New Hope, Pennsylvania of a reported suicide.

CLYDE. I had waited too long.

Tick Tock.

(**TERRY** *appears. Stares at* **CLYDE**.)

There was no conclusive evidence that it was suicide. But of course, the media says that, and then that's what it is forever.

BOWLBY. You don't think it was though?

CLYDE. No.

I thought it was an accidental overdose.

He swallowed too many doses of a particular pill he was prescribed. There was no note. Terry? Not leaving a note?? He – he was surrounded by his own writings. *None* mentioned suicidal thoughts or ideation.

Maybe I just like to think it was an accident though, I don't know.

BOWLBY. And so...? Were you betrayed? Disappointed?

CLYDE. Were you? When you found out?

BOWLBY. ...Yes. I didn't think it was an accident. I thought he said –

Fuck it.

CLYDE. I'm sorry to hear that.

BOWLBY. Don't get me wrong, I loved Terry a lot. I'm proud to say I knew him. And I couldn't do what he did. Few people can. Maybe it's the consequence of being brilliant? Of having a life like that?

CLYDE. I don't know if I believe that.

BOWLBY. What don't you believe?

CLYDE. I just miss him.

I feel lost.

I feel a revolution is coming.

BOWLBY. What do you mean?

CLYDE. I mean, I feel it inside of me. And he's the one calling me to it. Really. He's there in my mind. He's saying, Clyde, wake up. Wake up, man. Smell the roses, man. And then I think, I really think, what is it I'm supposed to be doing with my life?

TERRY. Revolution is not something fixed in ideology, nor is it something fashioned to a particular decade. It is a perpetual process embedded in the human spirit.

CLYDE. How do we live, Bowlby? That's what I always come back to is: how do we live?

NARRATOR #1. Disney, and his theme park conglomeration, surpassed the Yippies by a good fifty-five years.

NARRATOR #2. Since 1970, the park has expanded into six different theme parks worldwide, on three different continents.

NARRATOR #3. The reign of the Yippies, however, ended when the Vietnam War did.

NARRATOR #4. Perhaps without an impetus to respond to, the Yippies vanished.

NARRATOR #1. Some say the progressive ideology of this movement was swallowed up by mainstream culture.

NARRATOR #2. But others say, it just vanished.

NARRATOR #3. Disneyland's sixtieth birthday passed in July, a length of time that has spanned eleven presidential administrations.*

NARRATOR #4. And since then, the park has only been closed early on one other occasion: September 11th.

NARRATOR #1. But on that day in 1970...

NARRATOR #2. On that day...

> *(A moment, as the* **NARRATORS** *wait for* **BOWLBY**.*)*

BOWLBY. On that day two very different types of people met. And on that day, there was a chaotic result. But this chaos points to something, something I could never articulate until now...

Our lives encompass so many ways of living that no American is free of contradiction. But that fact, that fact shouldn't be looked at with disdain. I mean, isn't that one of our greatest achievements as a people, as a

---

*This line can be edited to reflect the most current count.

country? The fact that we live in a place that can hold opposing beliefs?

"The test of first-rate intelligence is the ability to hold two opposed ideas in mind at the same time and still retain the ability to function."

That's not Terry. That's F. Scott Fitzgerald.

And so, on that day, it ended with hardship, with blood, spilt blood, but still, I will tell you, I cannot look at that day without feeling a certain amount of

Pride.

> *(A moment, as the* **NARRATORS** *and* **BOWLBY** *breathe together, soaking in the Time.)*

End of Play

So why does a millennial write a play about Yippies?
An Afterthought
by Becca Schlossberg

It started at the 2009 revival of *Hair*.

(Maddy Parsigian, the director of our world premiere, got me the ticket and told me I would love the show so, in essence, all of this is really her fault.)

I sat inside the theater and watched a group of young, energetic rabble-rousers take the stage. As they danced back and forth, and back and forth, and went everywhere in the theater there was to go, I found myself entranced. At one moment in the show, the character of Woof looks out at the audience, his eyes circling all of the people in the theater, breathing us in, taking us truly in, and then he sings a song with a bunch of dirty words. I hadn't seen anything like it. Here was a celebration of life and love that I needed. I was in my first year of graduate school, and I was pretty miserable.

I grew my hair out and started reading. Then one day I was at my childhood home in New Jersey with my father. My family was/is a big Disney family. I went to Disney World twice. I grew up during the height of the Disney Renaissance. I could still recite *Beauty and the Beast* and *Aladdin* right here and now. It's one of my favorite party tricks. Hell, my father and I collected porcelain Disney figurines when I was a child.

He asked about my hair and my newfound affinity for hippies. He offhandedly said, as my father often does, "You know, Disney didn't like hippies. He threw them out of his park one time."

The only thing I remember feeling was the color. I was struck by a color in the idea of the event. It was exploding with color. I know that doesn't make sense, but that is the only real thing I can say about the idea, or the image of the day, when it was first planted into my mind.

Not shortly after I looked it up online. Sure enough, it had happened. And my dad had remembered. On a day in August of 1970, Disney had attempted to kick out hippies. But what was more remarkable, and what my dad hadn't quite remembered, was that the hippies actually "won" that day. They shut down the park. It was only the second time in history that had happened. It has only happened one other time since. Two hundred kids succeeded in doing something that still strikes me to this day as a fluke, an odd sort of modern miracle.

Some kind of metaphor for America emerged in my mind: two delusional forces at war with each other over a Fantasyland. From there, I dove deeper.

I read as much as I could. And like Bowlby, my protagonist, I became entranced with what I was finding. I was like a detective, tracking down a past that I longed to understand.

I watched some great movies and YouTube clips. And then I fell hard for Abbie Hoffman's words. Abbie's words lit my brain up. He was so poetic and fast and real and funny. Maybe it was my own dark Jewish sense of humor that connected me and him as well. Humor to Jews is a means of survival, a way in which we can carve lightness out of darkness and laugh even when there's not much to laugh at, and back then there didn't seem like a lot to laugh at. I loved the humor that the Yippies used. I had never seen anything like it and I don't think the world really has since then. Maybe because the idea of using satiric humor to crack on politicians has become so mainstream, but something about the combination of satire and in-your-face activism still jumps out at me as a unique form of protest.

And I also couldn't help but feel confronted with everything that I was finding. Confrontation isn't a bad thing, but it can make you feel uneasy. There were a lot of times where I could feel the conservative parts of me popping up, thinking, "Maybe that's a little too far," or,

"These people were daring and ballsy and all that, but what was it like to really be friends with them? Could they ever shut it off?"

Questions lead to more and more questions. It's a relief as a dramatist to know that I don't have to answer them, just point them out.

I got mostly through a rough draft my final year of graduate school. *Yippies* was to be my thesis. Then, during the first read-through, my adviser rejected it about forty pages in. Something about how the set couldn't be actualized. Something like that. To be honest, I blocked it out. It was pretty traumatic and unfair. I had spent far too many months working on the piece for it to be rejected in twenty minutes at the start of the school year.

I also should have fought for it more, but I didn't. I tried to meet with the professor and talk it out, but he was cold and aloof. So, I listened to my teacher. I let him kill my kid.

To this day, its probably one of the most devastating moments I have ever encountered as a student. So after that, I put it back on the shelf and went with another play for my thesis.

After that, pulling out the play felt too painful. I couldn't think about it for two years without feeling waves of regret and shame.

But then two years passed and it started to creep its way back into my brain. It's a good idea, I kept thinking, it would make a good play if I can get ahold of it.

Then I'd be on the phone with my mother. She'd ask about my playwriting. "What happened to *Yippies*?" she'd ask. "You should really go back to that. There's something there."

Some things can't be killed. And in the spring/summer of 2016, I couldn't shake it any longer. Some kind of newfound ambition or morbidity took hold of me. I'll do it very slowly, I reasoned. A half a page at a time. Slow and steady will win the race. Slow and steady was how I finally pulled the play from myself onto paper. Then, the further along I went, the more time I found myself writing. A goal of twenty minutes became forty, and then an hour, and then two hours. I found new resources and opened old ones. And to be fair, I think I did create something that's far better than anything I wrote initially. Maybe not the best way to bring about a better draft, but that's how it happened.

I reasoned that if the play ever lived to see the light of day, that would be part of its story. That would be a little piece of justice I could gain from finally willing the words onto paper.

Some things can't be killed. Not Yippies. Not history or its yellow pages. Not the spirit that lives inside of artists and activists that tells them to burn, burn, burn, and say the damn thing, and write the damn thing, and fight the fight that's worth fighting.

Lin-Manuel Miranda said that *Hamilton* reached out from beyond the grave and grabbed him. He wouldn't let go until his story was told. And I must confess I felt that way, too. These Yips planted seeds of something that I was able to unearth a good forty years after the fact, shaking me and moving me in ways I wouldn't have moved without them.

I hope this play will serve as a reminder of the fighting spirit that lives, dormant or not, inside all of us.